THE HOUSE THAT JACK BUILT

illustrated by

Rodney Peppé

DELACORTE PRESS/NEW YORK

For Christen

By the same author:
CIRCUS NUMBERS
THE ALPHABET BOOK

Originally published in England
by Longman Group Ltd

Copyright © 1970 by Rodney Peppé

Library of Congress Catalog Card Number: 78-112054

Printed in Great Britain

First American Edition: 1970

This is the house . . .

. . . that Jack built.

This is the malt

That lay in the house
that Jack built.

This is the rat,
That ate the malt

That lay in the house that Jack built.

This is the cat,
That killed the rat,
That ate the malt
That lay in the house
that Jack built.

This is the dog,

That worried the cat,
That killed the rat,
That ate the malt
That lay in the house
that Jack built.

This is the cow with the crumpled horn,

That tossed the dog,
That worried the cat,
That killed the rat,

That ate the malt
That lay in the house
that Jack built.

This is the maiden all forlorn,
That milked the cow
with the crumpled horn,
That tossed the dog,
That worried the cat,
That killed the rat,
That ate the malt
That lay in the
house that
Jack built.

This is the man  all tattered and torn,

That kissed the maiden all forlorn,
That milked the cow with the crumpled horn,
That tossed the dog,
That worried the cat,
That killed the rat,
That ate the malt
That lay in the house that Jack built.

This is the priest
all shaven and shorn,

That married the man all tattered and torn,
That kissed the maiden all forlorn,
That milked the cow with the crumpled horn,
That tossed the dog,
That worried the cat,
That killed the rat,
That ate the malt
That lay in the house
that Jack built.

This is the cock that crowed in the morn,

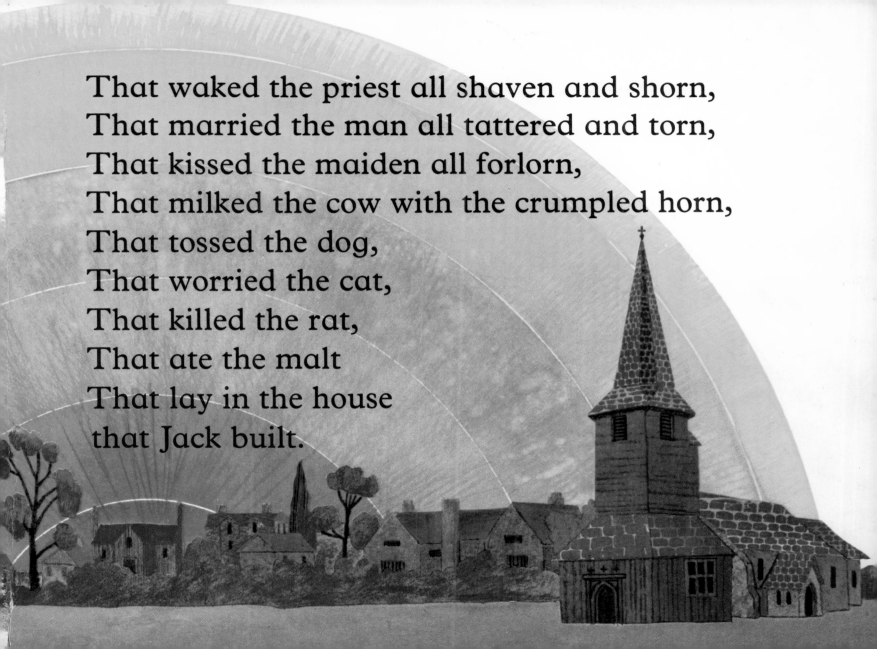

That waked the priest all shaven and shorn,
That married the man all tattered and torn,
That kissed the maiden all forlorn,
That milked the cow with the crumpled horn,
That tossed the dog,
That worried the cat,
That killed the rat,
That ate the malt
That lay in the house
that Jack built.

This is the farmer sowing his corn,

That kept the cock . . .

That waked
the priest . . .

That married
the man . . .

That kissed
the maiden . . .

That milked the cow . . .   That tossed the dog,

That worried the cat,

That killed the rat,

That lay in the house . . .

That ate the malt

. . . that Jack built.